I0615536

Wilhelm Hey

Picture Fables

Wilhelm Hey

Picture Fables

ISBN/EAN: 9783744792738

Printed in Europe, USA, Canada, Australia, Japan

Cover: Foto ©Andreas Hilbeck / pixelio.de

More available books at **www.hansebooks.com**

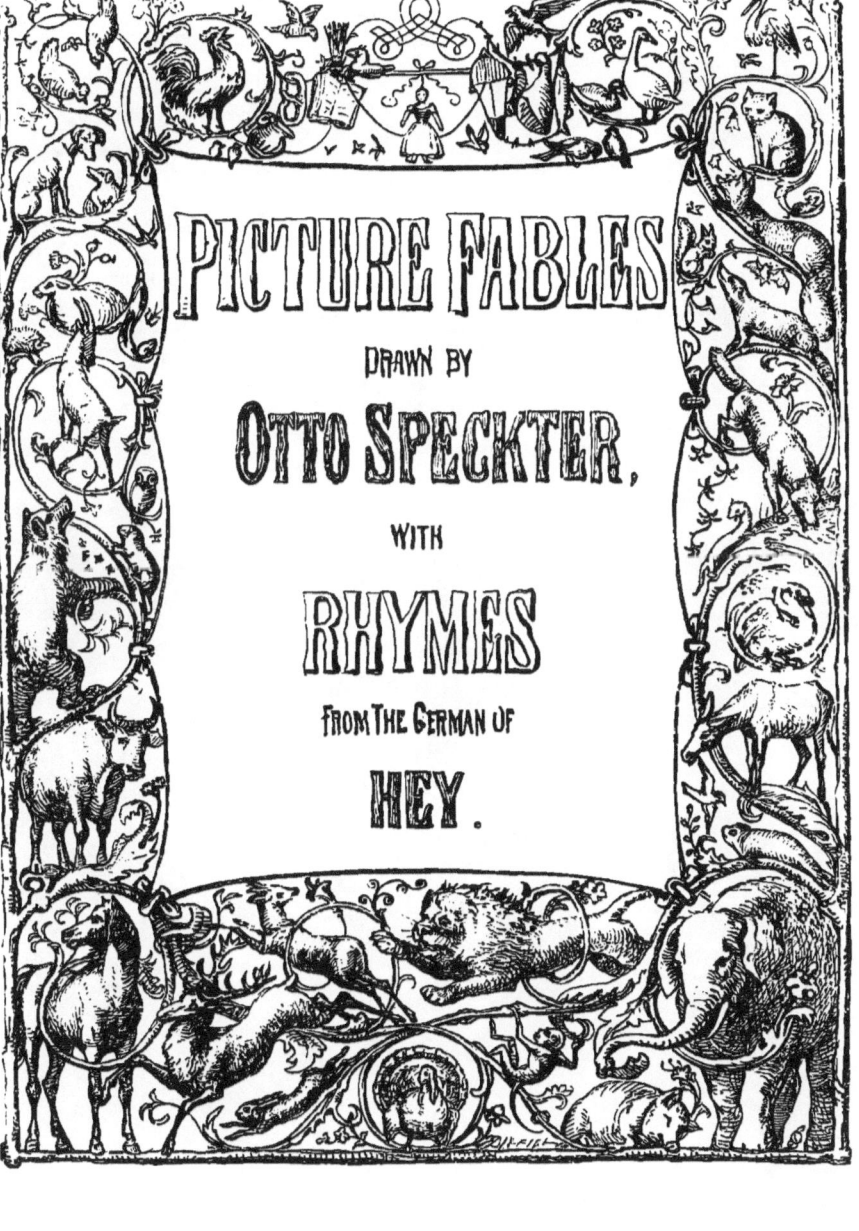

PICTURE FABLES

DRAWN BY

OTTO SPECKTER,

WITH

RHYMES

FROM THE GERMAN OF

HEY.

PICTURE FABLES,

DRAWN BY

OTTO SPECKTER,

ENGRAVED BY THE BROTHERS DALZIEL

WITH RHYMES

TRANSLATED FROM THE GERMAN OF F. HEY,

BY H. W. DULCKEN, Ph. Dr.

NEW EDITION.

LONDON:

ROUTLEDGE, WARNE, AND ROUTLEDGE,

FARINGDON STREET; AND WALKER STREET NEW YORK.

1863.

PREFACE.

— ◆ —

CHILDREN are naturally interested in the history of the Animal. Creation; every educated mother can bear testimony to the avidity with which the little ones listen to tales which have the cat and the dog, the lamb or the goat, for their heroes and heroines: it is therefore no matter of surprise that a work should be immensely popular which sets forth the adventures of these familiar favourites in simple pictures and verses, so short as not to fatigue the untutored mind.

The originals of this Picture Fable Book have been popular in every nursery and "Kinder Garten" (school for the young) in Germany for a score of years. And not in the nursery alone; the depth of thought and intense meaning conveyed in the beautiful designs of OTTO SPECKTER, combined with the sweet simplicity of the Rhymes of F. Hey, render the book fit for the matured intellect;—and it has consequently found a place among works of much higher pretension.

OTTO SPECKTER has drawn the pictures on the Wood. They have been engraved by the Brothers Dalziel expressly for this edition, which is now offered not only as a contribution to our juvenile literature, but as a work of art to children of the larger growth.

COME, all dear children, come quickly, do—
Here's goodly company waiting for you :
Living creatures from far and near
Are all together assembled here,
As though they all had so much to say,
And wish'd·to be question'd without delay.

There are dog and monkey, and ass and ox,
And stag and badger, and marmot and fox ;
There are birds and beasts, there are fishes too,
A crowd of visitors, all for you—
What the creatures say, would you like to know ?
Turn the page, little people : this book shall show.

THE RAVEN.

WHO's that beggar-man?—Come and see ;—
Black is his coat as black can be ;
At each door you may see him stay,
Asking food on a winter's day.
" Caw, caw," cries he, in a mournful tone ;
" Caw, caw, pray you give me a bone."

But the sweet spring-time soon began,
And blithe and gay was the beggar-man ;
Gladly he spread his black wings out,
O'er house and barn to roam about ;
And through the spring-time, in cheerful mood
He croak'd his thanks for the winter's food.

THE BIRD AT THE WINDOW.

PECK, peck, at the window—hark! what does he say?
"Just open a moment, good people, I pray;
The snow falls thick, and the wind blows rude,
And I'm almost frozen, and I 've no food.
Now pray let me in, good people, do,
And truly I'll always be thankful to you."

They let him in, at his time of need,
On the scatter'd crumbs on the floor to feed,—
For many a week did he there remain;
But when the warm sun was shining again,
The bird kept pining the whole day through,
So they open'd the sash, and away he flew.

2

SNOW MAN.

LOOK at the man there! Run, boys, quick!
See how he grasps his great thick stick;
Two whole days he's been standing so,
Yet he never hath struck one blow.
Snow Man, poor man, I'd scorn to be,
Holding a useless stick, like thee.

Snow Man, poor man, we truly may say,
Neither fighting nor running away.
Look at his face, it's all white and pale;
Don't shine too hotly, dear Sun, on the vale!
For if he but look on your bright warm ray,
Like water our Snow Man will vanish away.

3

BIRDS AT THE THRESHING-FLOOR.

"Out in the fields no food found we,
 Snow covers all things equally;
Then heard we your blows upon the ground,
And gladly came at the well-known sound;
Many a grain o'er the threshold flies,—
That's for us birds—and a welcome prize."

The men they kept time, one, two—one, two,—
And full and fuller the corn sacks grew;
There was corn enough for the house, and more,
For some little grains flew out at door.
But not for long on the ground they lay;
The birds soon spied them, and bore them away.

4

THE SQUIRREL AND THE WIND.

SQUIRREL. Ho, ho, Master Wind, with your noisy roar,
    I think I'd better go shut my door,
    And open another, there, over the way.
 WIND. I can blow in there, if I choose, to-day.
SQUIRREL. I'll shut them both, then, when you appear,
    For really I'd rather not have you here.

    You should see the face that the Wind then made,
    But the Squirrel cared not for all he said;
    The Wind kept shaking the old oak tree,
    The Squirrel scarce heard him—what cared he?—
    Over the fields he left him to roam,
    While he crack'd his nuts in his pleasant home.

THE BOY AND THE SQUIRREL.

Boy.   Squirrel, dear Squirrel, up there on the tree,
       You're perch'd up so high I scarce can see;
       Won't you come down now, with me to play?
Squirrel. It is too merry up here to-day;
       I think it far better fun, to go
       Here in the branches to and fro.

       Through the garden the child then stray'd;
       Through the branches the Squirrel play'd.
       Soon the boy came back to the tree—
       " Now, dear Squirrel, come play with me."
       But said Skuggy, " To tell you true,
       I haven't the time to play with you."

THE KITTENS.

KITTENS, now I'll find names for you,
Each from the thing it best can do:
Velvet we'll call the one there asleep,
Slyboots the kit who so softly can creep,
Mouser the pussy who hunting doth seem,
Lickdish the one with its nose in the cream.

They grew to be cats, each nice little kit.
Velvet all day on one's lap would sit;
In the corn-loft *Mouser* a-hunting would go,
While *Slyboots* crept through the barn below;
Lickdish went in the kitchen to dwell:
If he was a plague, ask cook,—she'll tell.

DOG AND CAT.

WHAT is it, Poodle? What can you see,
That you are barking so noisily?
Is it that Pussy's sitting up there,
And won't come down for your speeches fair?
Well, I think she is in the right;
If she came, you might chance to bite.

Pussy, she sat so long on the tree
Sleeping, as though a good dream had she;
Poodle, he would no longer wait,
But growling ran out at the garden gate;
Then Pussy she woke up quickly indeed,
And scamper'd away with the utmost speed.

BOY AND SWAN.

"LISTEN, you boy there among the trees,
  Just keep away from my children, please;
  And, sir, I'll beg you to drop that stone—
  I don't often speak in an angry tone;
  But you'd best run off, or I'll make you feel
  What a sturdy blow my wing can deal."

The cowardly boy ran off with speed,
  He fear'd the reward of his evil deed;
  The swan pursued, to increase his fear,
  But soon came back to his children dear.
  To tend his young gave him far more joy,
  Than thus to run after each idle boy.

SWAN AND CHILD.

"Wherefore are you, dear child, so shy?
  Neither wicked nor fierce am I;
  O'er the waters I gently glide,
  Make no ripple upon the tide;
  One thing only I have to say,
  Have you some bread to give away?"

Soon the child to the pond came on,
  Glad to see such a beauteous swan;
  How spotless white did his feathers glow,
  How gracefully swam he to and fro!
  And soon the child by the pond would stand,
  Feeding the swan from his little hand.

DOG AND KID.

Dog. Kid, I'll bite you, so now take care.

Kid. If you do, you will badly fare.

Dog. A very sharp set of teeth have I.

Kid. My horns are sharp,—should you like to try?

Dog. Kid, I was only joking with thee;
Let us play, and good friends we'll be.

Then all day they did leap and bound,
Chasing each other round and round;
When the doggie would bite too hard,
Kid would show where his horns appear'd.
Thus they play'd till the evening grey—
Who could merrier be than they!

PUG-DOG AND SPITZ.

PUG. Spitz, dear Spitz, for a moment come here;
        I'll ask you a secret, just lend me your ear,—
        Where have you hidden that beautiful bone,
        That no wicked thief may make it his own?
SPITZ. No, no, friend Pug, you'll not catch me so,
        The thief is the one who would want to know.

        Young Pug, he went sniffing and snuffing around,
        Till just by the stable the big bone he found;
        In his mouth already he grasp'd it tight,
        When he got his reward,—and it served him right.
        Master Spitz gave Pug such a tug by the ear,
        That the thief ran off yelping with pain and with fear.

HORSE AND SPARROW.

SPARROW. Horse, they have fill'd your trough, I see;
           Can you not spare a little for me?
           I only ask for a grain or two,
           And still there will be enough for you.
HORSE. I'll receive you, good bird, don't fear,
           For us both there is plenty here.

           Together they dined then, nothing loth,
           And, as he said, there was plenty for both;
           But when the summer sun shone warm,
           Then the flies came, a teasing swarm.
           But the sparrow caught all with ease,
           Who did not leave the good horse in peace.

13

THE ASS.

BOY. You lazy donkey, why don't you run?
         Just like a snail you go creeping on.
DONKEY. Don't beat me; I know I'm long on the road,
         But still I can fairly carry my load.
         Different servants our master doth need,
         Me for burden, the horse for speed.

         And the good old Ass, when his work was o'er,
         Went wearily in at the stable-door.
         There with the horse did he cosily dwell,
         Found there the supper he'd earn'd so well;
         On the clean straw his limbs did he lay,
         Slept there in quiet till break of day.

CHILD AND OX.

CHILD. Now what are you thinking of, Ox, I pray,
   That there you are lying, the livelong day,
   Making so grave and so learned a face?
 Ox. Thanks for the honour, that's not my case;
   Learning and books I must leave to you—
   I cannot *think*, I can only *chew*.

   For awhile the old Ox lay chewing there,
   Thinking of nothing, without a care,
   When the farmer harness'd him to the wain,
   To drag from the field a load of grain.
   And he did it bravely, and quickly too,
   But to *think* was a thing that he could not do.

THE LAMB.

"LAMB, why make you that plaintive moan?"
"Because my dearest mother is gone."
"Do you fear, poor thing, they would do you harm,
While she's away, that you're thus in alarm?"
"Fear! I don't know what you mean by fear,
Only I wish my mother were here."

The mother soon heard her young one's cry,
And came to the garden speedily;
Call'd it once with her gentle bleat,
Then ran the lambkin its mother to meet;
Swiftly over the grass it hied,
Close it press'd to its mother's side.

THE BIRD.

" Boy, I beg you with all my might,
Keep you out of my nestlings' sight ;
There is my nest—don't go too near—
For there are dwelling my children dear :
They'll be alarmed, and with fear they'll cry,
If you stare at them with your great round eye."

Though he wish'd to see where the nestlings lay,
The child still heedfully kept away ;
Over his nest the poor bird stood,
And spread his wings o'er his frighten'd brood,
And he look'd on the boy, with his eyes so mild,
" That you've not hurt them, I thank you, child."

THE TRAVELLER AND THE LARK.

TRAVELLER. Skylark, how early dost thou fly
              Joyously towards the sun on high?
SKYLARK. Blithely to God in heaven I sing,
              Thanks for life and for food to bring:
              This I've always been used to do;
              Traveller, is it your custom too?

              And as she sang in the air her song,
              And as he sturdily strode along,
              Both in their hearts were glad and gay,
              In the dear sun's bright, cheerful ray;
              And the good God in heaven above
              Heard all their songs of praise and love.

THE PIGEON.

Pretty Pigeon, the roof-tree upon,
Why are you cooing there, on and on,
Turning your head in that funny way?—
Pigeon. That is because I'm happy and gay;
For that to me, by God in heaven,
The light of the warm bright sun is given.

The Pigeon kept cooing, to tell his joy,
While sprang in his glee the merry boy—
Each rejoicing, as well he might,
In the beautiful sun that shone so bright.
And God, whose goodness had made them rejoice,
Was pleased at the sound of their joyful voice.

THE CANARY-BIRD.

Poor little bird, there you're lying, dead—
You can seek no more for a crumb of bread,
Your bright eye no longer can look on me,
You can't sit on my shoulder, gleefully;
And never more from your throat will ring
The joyous song you were wont to sing.

The children came, and in sorrow interr'd
In the pleasant garden the poor dead bird:
On its grave they planted a rose-bush, too,
Whereon the sweetest of buds soon grew;
And there sat the children many a day,
For they loved the spot where their favourite lay.

PAPER KITE AND BIRDS.

See you the great bird flying up there?
All you little ones, pray take care;—
For if you only come in his way,
He'll eat you up surely, without delay.
BIRD. Indeed, your great creature won't make me afraid;
It's only of painted paper made.

All on a sudden the brisk wind fell,
And down came the terrible bird, pell-mell!
The boys they tried and they tried in vain,
They never could get it up again;
But the little ones all, though no wind did blow,
Still flutter'd merrily to and fro.

BOY AND PUPPY.

BOY. Come, little Puppy, as quick as you can,
And learn to sit upright, just like a man.
PUPPY. What, young as I am, have I tasks to do?
Dear master, leave it a week or two.
BOY. No, Doggie, you'd best learn your lesson at once:
Who doesn't learn early, will still be a dunce.

So the dog had his lesson, it soon was done—
He could sit upright, or walk gravely on,
And he learn'd to swim o'er the stream so wide,
To fetch and to carry, and much beside.
And the boy, like his dog, to learn early began,
And became in due time, a wise, great man.

22

DOG AND CHILDREN.

"Dog, how is it that, great and strong,
  You yet are tormented all day long,
  And even forced in harness to go?"
Dog. Nobody else may use me so;
  But these are my master's sons, you see:
  From them I bear all things cheerfully.

Ere long came the dinner bell's welcome sound,
Then they untied him, the good old hound,
And to the dining-room took him away;
He wanted his dinner as well as they;
And each child for him a morsel would save,
But he liked that best which his master gave.

CHILD AND KITTEN.

"Kitty, Kitty, to scratch is wrong,—
    Don't stick out claws so sharp and strong;
    I want a paw soft, gentle, and mild."
Kitten. Yes, and I'll give you one, dear child;
    But it is right that I let you know,
    You should not pinch me and beat me so.

If the child pinch'd her by and by,
    Hurt poor Kitty, and made her cry;
    If Kitty's scratching was not good,
    And e'en if it brought a drop of blood,
    Nor Child nor Kitty did harm intend,
    And each continued the other's friend!

CHILD AND BOOK.

You dear little Book, come forth, my prize,
The people all say that you're so wise;
My father tells me, mamma says too,
That I may learn many things from you.
So now that I hold you to my ear,
Say what you know, Book, and let me hear.

Book, Book,—to speak do you still refuse,
Although you see I've no time to lose?
I want to run off, to jump and play,
And still not a single word you say:
Go, ugly Book, I don't like you, not I;
In the corner I'll throw you, there you may lie.

BIG DOLL AND LITTLE DOLL.

BIG DOLL. Dolly, unless you take pains, my dear,
You never will sit upright, that's clear;
You stretch your legs out so clumsily—
Can't you take pattern, my dear, by me?
DOLLY. I always try to; but here's the point,
I think they've made in my knees no joint.

The child she took them, and, laughing, cried,
"That quarrel shall soon be rectified;
Both you, dollies there, great and small,
Are stupid and senseless, after all."
Into the box she threw them again,
Where they together had often lain.

CAKE AND BREAD.

CAKE. Come hither, dear child, my name is Cake:
   I taste very sweet; 't is me thou must take.
   That yonder is Bread, in its plain brown dress;
   Men scarce will eat it in dire distress.
BREAD. Go, take him, my child, I do not care,
   To-day or to-morrow to me you'll repair.

   The child had a long, long walk to take,
   He had no money to buy him cake;
   In due time hunger began to come,
   He was glad to eat bread when he got home;
   How thankful even for that we grow,
   If once of hunger the pains we know.

LITTLE MOUSE.

LADY.   Wherefore, dost thou, little Mouse,
          Steal the sugar in my house?
MOUSE. Dearest lady, oh forgive,
          I've four children where I live:
          Very hungry still are they;
          Let me have it, lady, pray.

          The lady look'd on with friendly eyes,
          And said, " Well, Mouse, you may keep your prize;
          For I am going, just like you,
          To feed my child, who is hungry too."
          So Mousie ran off—with, oh ! what speed—
          And the lady went gaily her child to feed.

POODLE.

" Who's been taking my milk without leave?
Had I but caught him, the naughty thief——
Poodle, can you have taken some?
Poodle, Poodle, why don't you come?
That fine white beard, pray, where did you get,
And say, good Poodle, how came it wet?"

The lady saw him, and laugh'd loud out,
" Ah, Poodle, Poodle, what are you about?
It can't be you that so greedy has grown."
Oh, then Poodle's tail fell drooping down,
And he howl'd, and whined, and was so ashamed,
I don't think again for theft he'll be blamed.

DOG AND HEDGEHOG.

Dog. Hark ye, Hedgehog, I'll seize you there.
Hedgehog. Hark ye, Doggie, I do not care.
Dog. Tell me how can you yourself defend?
Hedgehog. My prickles will teach you that, my friend;
I have been seized by many a one,
Who soon was sorry for what he'd done.

Doggie seized him, but ah, too fast!
"Bow! what a prickly skin thou hast!
For one to stroke you it is not good;
You prick one at once, and bring the blood."
Doggie a doleful visage drew,
"Go along, Hedgehog, I don't like you."

ROCKING-HORSE AND HOBBY-HORSE.

ROCK. Ha! how manfully I can spring,
    Up and down with a ceaseless swing!
 HOB. How I bound with my master—what fun!—
    Through the garden with ceaseless run.
CHILD. Good horses, make not that boastful noise,
    For, after all, you're but wooden toys.

  On one through the garden rode he about,
  Till that his legs were quite wearied out;
  Then on the back of the other sat he,
  And swung himself up, 'twas a sight to see;
  But all was done when he went away:
  There, in the corner, quite still stood they.

RABBITS.

How happy you rabbits seem to be,
Sitting together so merrily;
And looking around you, in cheerful mood.
RABBITS. We're happy because our master's so good;
Each day he visits us thrice, or more,
And fresh leaves brings us, a bounteous store.

They heard a light footstep come to the gate,
And each little ear was prick'd up straight;
A head was seen, and a friendly hand.
That were both well known to the little band;
A bounteous shower of leaves did fall,
And soon they were merrily nibbling, all.

BOY AND BUTTERFLY.

Boy. Little pretty butterfly,
  Roaming through the air so high,
  Tell me now, whereon live you,
  As you fly the garden through.
Butt. Blossom-scent, and sunshine fair,
  Are the food for which I care.

  The boy would have caught the butterfly,
  But that it begg'd so piteously,
  " Dear boy, do me no grievous ill ;
  Let me play in the sunshine still.
  Ere it hath pass'd, the evening red,
  I shall be lying, cold and dead."

           F

BOY AND BIRD.

Boy. Now I shall grasp thee, bird so bright;
Bird. Dost thou grasp me?   Then hold me tight.
Boy. Oh that's naughty, bird, of thee,
     Thus to have flown upon the tree.
Bird. Haste thee a pair of wings to buy,
     Then thou canst come there as quick as I.

The bird sat safely upon the tree,
While the boy was watching him wistfully.
At first he was vex'd, but not for long;
For he thought, "After all, it is not wrong,
That the bird on the tree should like best to sing,
While in freedom down here I can run and spring."

BIRDS AND OWL.

BIRDS. D' ye come to the light once, old Mother Owl ;
        Don't look about with that doleful scowl.
        By night you are able to scare us away,
        But let us just tease you a little by day.
OWL. Were it not that the sun so brightly shone,
        I'd soon make an end of you, every one.

        The others play'd on ; she sat sulking still,
        Till one of them ask'd, " Pray, are you ill,
        Your face is dark as a stormy day ? "
        She said, " I'm angry to see you play ;
        I'm sorry the sun comes shining through,
        And I hate your questions, your noise, and you."

BAT AND BIRD.

BAT. Now come to me, dear birdie, do,
    And let me be friendly and play with you.
BIRD. I never with you have friendship made;
    To look at your face it makes me afraid.
BAT. Ah, poor little I;—thus I knew 't would be:
    Not a mouse nor a bird will play with me.

And so the poor bat sat all alone,
To be her comrade there was not onc;
To the darkest corner away she fled,
And none could tell where she made her bed.
Late in the evening came she out,
Drearily flutter'd the housetops about.

COCKS.

" SEE you that strange cock scampering there?
I've taught him a lesson, I hereby declare.
Always into my yard he'd come,
As if it had been his proper home;
Remember, whoever troubles me
Shall be turn'd out quickly and shamefully."

Master cock was so fierce and so given to strife,
He led fowls and geese a most terrible life;
If ever a stranger appear'd in his yard,
He abused him in language insulting and hard,
But one day, when on dog Spitz he fell,
That brave dog caught him and shook him well.

BEAR.

WHO is that dancing-master there ?
Welcome, welcome, you wonderful bear !
What a number of tricks you know !
How gracefully on your hind legs you go !
But one thing, Bruin, spoils all the play—
You grumble in such an ill-temper'd way.

For the bear indeed it was no great fun,
To have to keep dancing when once he'd begun ;
He wish'd himself back in the woods again,
To sleep at ease in his cozy den.
Here, hungry for half the day was he ;
He'd rather go rob the honey bee.

THE DANCING MARMOT.

" You'll give me a trifle, good people, I'm sure;
I'm very unhappy, and wretched, and poor.
My friends in the corn-field are merry and gay,
While I am here hopping and dancing for pay;
In winter they sleep without danger or dread,
While I must be waking and begging for bread."

" I pity you much, you poor little thing;
I too love to gambol, to dance, and to spring;
But had I to dance at another's behest,
'T would not seem to me like a game or a jest.
For you 't was, poor marmot, a sorrowful day,
When cunning men caught you, and took you away."

THE SOW.

" CHILDREN," said the Mother Sow,
" Mind you listen to me, now—
You must be neat, and you must be clean,
Always look tidy and fit to be seen;
You're not to go stumping through all the town,
You're not in each puddle to lay you down."

But just what the sow had accustom'd them to,
And just what they always noticed her do,
That learned the children every one,
And all did just as their mother had done—
And from her example, each became
A pig in deed, and a pig in name.

TURKEY-COCK AND YOUNG ONES.

" COME, all you children, attend to me,
  Mind you behave yourselves peacefully ;
  It's very naughty, that angry mood :
  This very instant be cheerful and good.
  Your strife and your clamour must be appeased,
  Else, children, remember, I shall be displeased."

Now into the yard, by some strange hap,
  A boy there came, with a scarlet cap ;
  And oh, the old Turkey grew furious quite,
  And scream'd, " Take the cap away from my sight."
  But the boy said, laughing, and still march'd on,
" Sir Turkey, what harm may my cap have done ?"

                                G

FOX AND DUCK.

"FRIEND Duck, on the pond, why swim you there?
 Won't you for once to the shore repair?
 I have a question to ask of you."
DUCK. Sir Fox, I could teach you nothing new,
 You're altogether too clever for me;
 So I'd rather remain where I am, you see.

Sir Fox went strolling along the shore,
Ill pleased was he, as he thought it o'er:
He only wish'd she would come in his clutch,
But the sly little Duck had suspected as much;
And to catch her that day was too hard for him:
"Oh dear," he thought, "if I could but swim!"

STAG.

" HARK! 'tis the hunting horn I hear,
There are the dogs too, terribly near;
Yes, and the hunters behind yon tree—
No time here to be lost, I see;
Running is now the best I can do,
To trust to my legs to bring me through."

The dog rush'd after with all his might—
" Soon, Master Stag, I shall hold you tight."
But the old Stag said, " My friend, have a care;
Here's a ditch, I shall leap it—there,
Take care how you follow, or you may rue,
It's rather too wide, I fancy, for you."

PUG AND HOUND.

Pug. I wouldn't be you, and have to run
      All day through rain and through tempest on.
Hound. I wouldn't be you, to have to keep
      All day in the dusty room asleep.
Pug. On the warm sofa they'll let me be.
Hound. Running and leaping's the fun for me.

      Our Hound he ran on o'er mountain and wold,
      Never caring for heat or cold;
      To keep in the house Pug thought 'twas best,
      So all the morning he took his rest;
      But wheezy and fat he quickly grew,
      And panted with pain at each breath he drew.

44

HORSE AND FOAL.

" RUN along, Foal, my sportive child,
  Swift as the wind, and as free and wild;
  Play while the day for sport doth last—
  When you are great, the good time is past;
  Then you have work and trouble enow,
  To carry the rider, to drag the plough."

The sportive Foal gallop'd far and wide,
  In freedom and joy, by its mother's side;
  It had but to gambol early and late,
  And thus it became strong, handsome, and great.
  When, three years after, I saw it again,
  'T was able to draw the heaviest wain.

CHICKEN.

Chicken! Chicken! silly child, stay,
Whither art running so quickly away?
Always prying each corner through,
Ever searching for something new;
But when your mother is out of sight,
You'll cry with terror, you foolish wight.

The chicken into the garden ran,
But to cry with terror it soon began;
The mother soon heard its plaintive cry,
And sought for it long and anxiously;
Half dead with fear, it crept 'neath her wing,
And thought, "Ne'er again I'll do such a thing."

LITTLE FISH.

Little Fish, little Fish, listen to me,
Watch not the bait there so greedily;
'T will enter your neck with a cruel sting,
'T will tear you sorely, you foolish thing;
See you not there, on the bank, the man?
Little Fish, little Fish, flee while you can.

Little Fish thought he knew better than we:
He saw the bait, and nought else saw he;
The boy on the bank, he said, (he knew best,)
Was only sitting down there to rest.
He gave one snap at the tempting bait,
And then he struggled—but all too late.

BOY AND DUCK.

Boy. Now, good old Duck, just tell to me
The number of this your family.
Duck. I've not learn'd to count, I grieve to say,
But do not think you can take one away;
I keep them carefully all, dear Boy,
For each of them gives me the greatest joy.

She call'd them all, in a motherly tone,
And round they came trooping, every one;
She look'd, with a mother's joy and pride,
On the little creatures that swam by her side;
Away o'er the pond she led her brood,
And watching them long the young boy stood.

STORKS.

CHILD. Now tell me, dear Storks, what do you intend,
   That towards the sunlight your way you wend?
STORKS. All around us is cold and drear,
   Therefore we hasten away from here.
CHILD. Then fly away on your light wings, fly,
   But mind you come back, Storks, by and by.

Few days had pass'd since the Storks had flown,
Before the winter came driving on;
He saw their nest, on the roof-tree old,
And piled it with snow-feathers, white and cold;
And oh, 't was a bleak and a cheerless nest:
No stork there in comfort could take his rest.

STORKS.

" THE sun shines bright, the summer's near,
And, as we promised, we Storks are here;
Though we were compell'd afar to roam,
We forgot not the nest we'd left at home.
I see it still clings where last year it stood;
We'll clean it, and live there, and raise our brood."

With straw and with wood did they mend it well,
How gladly they labour'd no tongue can tell;
Dame Stork during three weeks sat thereon,
Then heard the neighbours a piping tone.
There were six little Storks, a noisy brood,
Who open'd their hungry bills for food.

HAM AND SAUSAGE.

HAM. Sausage, there in the pan, can you tell
    What is it makes this wonderful smell?
SAUSAGE. I can explain it, I opine:
    The beautiful smell you perceive is mine;
    They 've put me here on the fire to roast,
    And I smell like a nosegay of flowers, almost.

    But soon our sausage became so warm,
    It greatly fear'd it would come to harm.
    " Cook, where do you loiter so long?" it said,
    " The fire is scorching me, I 'm afraid.
    Why don't you turn me, you stupid Cook?
    I'm burnt quite black in the face—just look!"

HARE.

MARK the conceited hare, there, do—
Sits he not up like a hero true?
Proudest glances around he throws;
Proudly perks up his little nose;
Thinks, if a foeman to him should come,
He quickly would send him, beaten, home.

If all alone in the world were he,
He 'd be a hero, undoubtedly.
But now he but heard the crack of a whip,
And at once his courage gave him the slip;
Without once stopping to glance around,
Off he ran with a skip and a bound.

MILK-JUG AND WATER-PAIL.

MILK-JUG. Water-pail, how can we two agree?
　　　　　What are you, pray, sir, compared to me?
　　　　　You'd better be gone, to drudge about,
　　　　　For, if you stay, I shall turn you out.
WATER-PAIL. My dear little Jug, mind what you do;
　　　　　Fine things are brittle, and so are you.

　　　　　The milk-jug thought always of his worth,
　　　　　He look'd so handsome upon the hearth;
　　　　　But the cook she crack'd him, which made him leak,
　　　　　And he lay on the dust-bin that very week;
　　　　　But the plain old water-pail held his own
　　　　　Full three years after the jug fell down.

THE CAT IN THE SNOW

" Pussy, you lift your paws so high,
  And look down on them so ruefully,
  To your neck almost you sink in the snow.
  It's cold, is it not, down there to go?
  Would not your walking be better done
  If a pair of good stout boots you'd on?"

She didn't wear boots, our good little cat,
  But she march'd on bravely, in spite of that.
  Through the snow she whisk'd at the barn-door in;
  Where she shook, and she lick'd her paws quite clean.
  And she caught no cold, but sprang merrily
  To the highest beam of the old root-tree.

CHICKENS.

" Say, little Chickens, why run ye
    Thus to your mother, in noisy glee?
    Some good treasure now hath she found,
    Some little worm that crawl'd on the ground;
    Making her now so eagerly call,
    That you may come and partake of it, all ! "

    The good old hen, she was glad indeed,
    To see all her children around her feed ;
    With joy she look'd on the merry train,
    And sought to content them, with might and main ;
    Not one piece for herself took she,
    Till all had been cared for, equally.

SWALLOW AND SPARROW.

SWALLOW. Sparrow, Sparrow, what are you about?
SPARROW. I wanted a nest, and I've found one out.
SWALLOW. But, Sparrow, this nest is mine, you see.
SPARROW. Well, then in future 'twill be for me.
SWALLOW. Sparrow, Sparrow, you wicked thief,
           Do you not fear you will come to grief?

           The Swallow thought, "I am cheated, 'tis true,
           But I can soon build me a nest, anew;
           Plenty of clay and of twigs can be found,
           And I have a bill that is sturdy and sound;
           I'll build me a nest for the one he has ta'en,
           And to-morrow at eve I'll be settled again."

CAT.

Pussy, Pussy, creeping so sly,
Over the housetops ever so high ;
You see the swallow that's sitting there,
You want to seize him before he's aware.
He'll fly, good Pussy, and quickly too ;
You want to know him, but he knows you.

Angry and cross was our Puss that day.
As the bird on his light wing sped away,
She thought, " How strange that he flies, that swallow,
Up in the air where I can't follow."
But Puss soon forgot it, and roam'd through the house,
And caught what was better for her—a mouse.

I

FROG.

" IT's chilly and cold in the water, down there,
I'm glad to escape to the warm upper air
I'll sit me down on the broad grey stone,
And bask in the sunshine, all alone ;
With wide mouth gaping, I'll here recline,
And thank the sun that on me doth shine."

But who leans there on the bridge's rail ?
The Frog, of that boy can tell a tale,—
How he's flung at him many a stone,
And if one of them hit, 'twould all be done.
And soon as the Frog that boy can see,
He plumps in the water, speedily.

CHILD AND DOVE.

CHILD. Dove, I'm sure you must be distrest,
     Dragging the feathers thus from your breast.
DOVE. It hurts me, truly, but nought I care,
     If I make but a nest that's soft and fair,
     Wherein my little ones, safe from harm,
     May lie and be shelter'd snug and warm.

     Then thought the Child, " Like the Dove that's here,
     So careful is every mother dear ;
     So anxious to care for her children's good,
     Lest they want for shelter, or warmth, or food ;
     With my own mother the same I see,
     The best that she has she gives to me."

KEEPER.

BOY. Keeper, wilt go out walking, sir?
DOG. I'd like to go, but I may not stir.
BOY. Why not? We go but a step or two;
    Come, good Doggie, and we'll take you.
DOG. No, no, the house would be left alone,
    And a thief could enter while we were gone.

    As they went out, at the door he lay,
    And look'd at both in a friendly way;
    Then he ran carefully all around,
    To see that the house was safe and sound.
    When they came home, he ran with might,
    And met them with joy, for he'd done what was right.

GOAT.

" Nanny Goat, Nanny Goat, let me know
Why your beard and your horns do grow."
" I have a beard, that pull it you may,
So long as with me I let you play.
I have two horns to make you flee,
Whenever that pastime suits not me."

" We'll soon see that, friend," the boy laugh'd out,
And he pull'd the goat by its beard so stout ;
But he pull'd too hard, and up rose she,
And butted him soundly—" Oh dear ! " cried he.
But soon his anger had pass'd away,
And he brought her, for supper, a bundle of hay.

SEAL AND SEAGULL.

SEAL.   Were I like you, Bird, light airy thing,
          How soon to the sun my way I'd wing.
SEAGULL. To go there, at first, was my intent,
          But I found I was wrong, as upward I went ;
          Still as I mounted, it colder grew,
          So I left the sun, and came back to you.

          " Colder up there—and yet warms us here ! "
          'T was too hard for the seal to make it clear ;
          On the ice he stretch'd him and ponder'd thereon,
          And lay there and slept till the daylight was gone.
          If he had any dreams as there he was lying,
          They were of the warm sun, I'm sure, and of flying.

LION AND DOG.

LION, mighty and strong is thy frame—
Men tremble and quake at the sound of thy name;
In the forest no creature can combat thy rage,
And threat'ning art thou even here in thy cage.
But the little dog thou permittest still
To bite thee, and tease thee, as much as he will.

LION. I am a prisoner, lone and forlorn,
From all my brothers and sisters torn;
They put the cur dog into my den:
I was glad to behold any creature then;
I gave him his life, without demur,
And I've something to love me, if 't is but a cur.

HARE.

" See you nothing, little Hare,
Stirring in the thicket there?
Prick your long ears bolt upright,
Or you'll be in sorry plight;
'Tis a hunter—run, Hare, run!
Here he comes, and has a gun."

The hare twitch'd his long ears to and fro,
And ran as quickly as he could go;
Before the hunter could take his aim,
He found that, for once, too late he came.
In vain he shot off the gun so tall;
It cost him his powder, and that was all.

APE AND BOOTS.

" Boots, ah, Boots, I have always seen
How men so gallantly walk therein.
For once, I think, I will try them too ;
And walk up and down in them, men, like you.
Were some of you only here to see,
How you would admire and envy me."

But hark ! in the thicket, a noise, good Ape ;
The hunter is coming, and you must escape.
Now draw off your boots without delay,
And climb through the tall trees, up and away.
But the boots are sticky, you cannot flee ;
No, you 're caught, poor Ape, through your vanity.

κ

BEAR AND BEEHIVE.

"HERE'S a beautiful smell! how sweet!
Here with honey I'm sure to meet;
But here all the nasty bees are, too.
I should like to learn from some one who knew,
Why always they're buzzing about my ears
Wherever a honey-hive appears."

He knew he'd found honey, the sly old bear,
But a threat'ning swarm of bees was there;
He call'd up his most courageous mood,—
"I'll get it," he said, "it *is* so good:"
Oh, but the little bees stung him sore,
Till he grumbled, "I'll ne'er eat honey more."

BOY AND FOAL.

Boy. Come, Foal, and let me your back bestride ;
      Up hill, down dale, we'll merrily ride.
Foal. No, Boy, my step is for you too fast,
      I surely should throw you off at last ;
      There stands in the corner a horse for you,
      Who'll bear you more safely than I could do.

      He stretch'd forth his arms, its neck to clasp,
      But, swift as the wind, it eluded his grasp ;.
      He pouted at first, but soon bestrode
      His wooden horse, and thereon he rode,
      But said, " I'm determined, come what may,
      I'll ride on that pony, some fine day."

CHICKENS.

"Chickens! what may the matter be?
 That you're all running so timidly;
 See you him lurking, the fox so sly.
 You need not fear, and I'll tell you why,—
 Our watch-dog has seen his crafty face,
 And will send him packing in dire disgrace."

The fowls from that day were scared no more—
 The good dog Keeper he kept the door—
 Cackling they went through the yard all day,
 And many an egg in the straw laid they;
 At night they quietly slept in stall,
 For good dog Keeper, he watch'd for all.

ELEPHANT.

CHILD. Elephant, sturdy and strong art thou,
    A hundred men can scarce make thee bow,
    And thou dost allow us children still
    To question and tease thee as much as we will.
    All things thou dost at thy master's command,
    And art pleased at the touch of his patting hand.

ELEPHANT. I scarcely know how the thing befell,
    But that they caught me I know full well;
    And men, though they be not strong and tall,
    Are *clever*, and that's worth more than all.
    My master keeps me, and feeds me each day,
    And thus his behest I gladly obey.

WEASEL.

CHILD. Weasel, where run you so hurriedly?
WEASEL. Home to my child, who's waiting for me.
CHILD. What is that in your mouth, I beg?
     Does it not look almost like an egg?
     I see, now, your thievish life you'd save;
     That's why you run so, egg-stealing knave!

The cunning weasel was nearly lost,
For the boy had caught him once, almost;
As the weasel ran, he follow'd fast,
But the knave slipp'd in at his hole at last.
For the boy the hole was too narrow, though,
So for once he allow'd the thief to go.

FOX AND COCK.

Fox. Who's clever enough, now, my riddle to guess?
Cock. Come, ask me, I *think* I shall know, I confess.
Fox. He has a head, with cunning replete;
      He has a mouth, that always would eat;
      Now he comes running and seizeth thee.
Cock. Ah me, the villain! he's eating me.

      Poor Cock! but he who would be so wise,
      Should have known, that danger in wisdom lies;
      Knowing the fox, he should not have tried
      To guess the riddles the cheat supplied.
      Sorry was he for the boast he'd made,
      When for his wit with his life he paid.

CHILD AND SWALLOW.

" How glad I am, your long journey o'er,
Dear little Swallow, to see you once more.
Say, who, in the far land, taught you to know,
That Spring would return, and 't was time to go ? "
" It was God that taught me—He knoweth best,
The time to roam, and the time to rest."

And far as she 'd flown, to the distant clime,
Not once had the swallow miss'd her time ;
The snow had melted, the sun shone warm,
There danced in its ray the gnat's gay swarm.
Daintily then did the swallow fare,
For her and her young there was food, and to spare.

GREYHOUND AND TURNSPIT.

GREY. Queer little Doggie, how small are you,
    And how crooked your legs are, too.
TURNS. Your shape is slender, your legs are long,
    But you're a coward—your *heart's* not strong.
GREY. I can catch the hare, when he runs his best.
TURNS. I can drive the fox from his cunning rest.

    The huntsman bade them to hold their peace,
    When the chase commenced their talk must cease.
    And oh, the big greyhound ran fleetly then,
    And the little dog routed the fox from his den ;
    Great one and little, each in his way,
    Earn'd the praise of the master that day.

L

STAG.

" I am so great, and noble, and high,
    Two terrible branching horns have I ;
    Then why should I fear, whate'er betide,
    Why from the dogs should I run and hide ?
    I 'll wait for them boldly, and here at bay,
    Prove which is bravest, I or they."

There he stood, boastful and brave ;—but hark !
    A sound in the distance was heard, like a bark ;
    Oh then, on a sudden, he changed his mind,
    And I saw him run off, as fleet as the wind.
    And when he crouch'd down in his covert green,
    He 'd quite forgotten how brave he 'd been.

SWANS.

Why, pretty Swans, do you always go
On the water thus, to and fro?
Swans. Our limbs are weak, and we cannot spring,
Our voices are harsh, and we cannot sing;
Our only pleasure must therefore be,
To sail together in amity.

You're right, dear Swans, together to keep;
And though I can dance, and sing, and leap,
I never should care for play or for song,
If no one were with me all day long.
Singing together makes song sound gay;
Meetings make mirth. and playmates, play.

DOLL.

"Have I not, Dolly, enough to do,
　To teach such a stupid thing as you?
　Clever and wise I would have you grow:
　I teach you all that you ought to know;
　And when the teaching and trouble are o'er,
　You're the stupid Dolly you were before."

Thus Dolly was scolded, and yet didn't cry,
　For the child hardly meant it seriously.
　She knew that poor Dolly meant to be good,
　And gladly would learn, if she only could;
　But scolding and punishment well they earn,
　Who want not the pow'r, but the will, to learn.

BOY AND ASS.

" Ass, I will give you a riddle to-day :
    What is that creature that's brownish or grey,
    That hasn't much brain, but long ears to his head,
    That cries Eh-haw! and goes with a lumb'ring tread.'
Ass. My Boy, that's too deep and too hard for me;
    What kind of an animal may that be?

    Then the boy laugh'd loudly, and cried, as he went,
    " Oh shame on you, Donkey! 'twas you I meant."
    He heard, but he never could tell, they say,
    Why the boy thus angrily went away.
    The foolish boy, how came it to pass,
    That he ask'd such a question—of an ass?

FOX AND GOOSE.

Fox. Dame Goose, the sun shines cheerfully;
    Won't you go out for a walk with me?
Goose. Master Fox, I'd rather not go with you,
    I was thinking the sun shone brightly too;
    But since that before my door you stay,
    All the fine weather seems past, and away.

    'T was not that the weather was bad, no—no—
    There was not a storm of rain, or of snow;
    But the old Goose would not go,—not she,
    For she knew the Fox and his knavery.
    Had she walk'd with him down the lane,
    He'd hardly have brought her safe home again.

CANARY-BIRD AND HEN.

CANARY. Be quiet there, Hen, with your cackling voice,
How can our master put up with your noise?
HEN. I certainly cannot sing like you,
My cackling is harsh and hoarse, 'tis true;
But look at my eggs with their pure white shell,
And then wonder why all people like me so well.

Who is to settle this quarrel, pray?
Each is excellent in its way;
The Canary to live in his cage on the wall,
In the farmyard the Hen with her cackling call.
What both of them give us will pleasant appear,
The egg for the mouth, and the song for the ear.

SPARROW IN THE SNOW.

Boy. Bird, how the wintry wind doth blow;
    Art not frozen, in ice and snow?
Sparrow. I can be gay, e'en in winter-time,
    My feather coat guards me in ev'ry clime;
    Cheerfully to and fro I fly:
    Dress as you will, you're not warmer than I.

    Then thought the boy, "I should do so too,
    Cold winter should bring me but courage new;
    I, like the sparrow, am warmly dress'd,
    To run and to play, spite of cold, were best."
    So he cared not for frost and cold, so long
    As they left him healthy, and brave, and strong.

DOG AND RAVEN.

"Raven, you thief—here—stop, I say,
You're taking my fine bit of meat away!"
"Pray, little Dog, just keep the peace,
D'ye know, I belong to the new police?
And, taking the booty from those who steal,
As they've dealt by others, by them I deal."

What the raven said, was, I think, not true,
When with the dog's dinner away he flew.
But the dog didn't tell of him anywhere:
The truth is, I think, he did not dare;
He'd rather not tell them, on the whole,
How he came by the meat the raven stole.

M

PUPPIES.

Now, Spitz, I think it but right and fair,
That each of your young ones a name should bear,
For such has the custom been, alway;
I don't think it requisite, I must say,
For when to them, "Come, my dears!" I cry,
They hear me at once, and at once reply.

And when the mother did but look round,
The pups came to her with playful bound.
But when they older grew, then came
The people and gave to each a name;
And the dogs knew quickly their master's call,
And learn'd to follow them, one and all.

ROD.

CHILD. Bad Rod, how shall you punish'd be,
      For all the trouble you've caused to me
  ROD. To quarrel with me, dear child, is vain;
      It was for your good I caused you. pain.
CHILD. So they say, but it hurt, I know;
      Go you away, you bad Rod, go.

      With eyes of anger she look'd thereon,
      And thought, " Could it but be for ever gone."
      And, when each counsel and warning word
      That her mother spoke, she with meekness heard,
      The Rod from the glass soon vanish'd away;
      I've even heard it was burnt one day.

BUTTERFLY.

" Butterfly, Butterfly, flitting away,
  Shaking your bright wings, so radiant and gay,
  Nearer the candle, and yet more near;
  Poor little Butterfly, can you not hear?
  You'll burn to a cinder your painted wing,
  And die in anguish, poor heedless thing."

  The child felt sad for the butterfly,
  So he caught it swiftly and daintily;
  He set it out on the window-sill,—
  There, through the night it felt frosty and chill;
  But on it the morning sunbeams fell,
  And it flutter'd away, quite strong and well.

ROES.

" WE'RE little roes, one, two, three, four,
Merrily tripping the greenwood o'er ;
Jumping and capering, every one,
Fighting together, but only in fun.
Here there is nobody in the way,
Huntsman or hound, to disturb our play."

Just then, past them a peasant strode,
Sturdily stepping along the road,—
They saw him, but thought,—" He's far off still,
And scarcely likely to do us ill."
But when he was passing their meadow o'er,
They ran off, fleet as the wind, all four.

THIEF AND DOG.

THIEF. Down, Doggie, down, raise no alarm,
I haven't come here to do you harm;
Look at this sausage, there, take it now.
DOG. No, no, that's just why I bark—bow, wow.
You have come here to steal, I see;
That's why you're friendly and kind to me.

He bark'd, the good dog, with all his might,
Till it rang out far through the silent night;
Till it roused the people who sleeping lay,
And the wicked thief slunk baffled away.
And good care he took to come no more;
Then the dog lay down, for the danger was o'er.

CHILD AND BEE.

CHILD. Go away, go away, naughty Bee,
   Leave me, I tell you, instantly.
   You want to give me a sting, I know.
 BEE. Let me speak, and don't scold me so ;
   You're always with me so angry and cross,
   If I gave no honey, you'd feel the loss.

   Now, when the child thought the matter o'er,
   He scolded the busy bee no more ;
   But saw how it hover'd the flowers about,
   Sucking from each the sweetness out.
   And all his fear of the sting lost he,
   In praising the insect's industry.

BADGER.

Badger, you think you're lying there,
Safe and sound in your den—beware !
Here come some who will make you smart :
Come out and show if you've a heart ;
I know not if pleasant it will appear,
To have the dogs barking so close to your ear.

The dogs fell on him with bark and with yell ;
He fought like a brave badger, fiercely and well.
But amid the bravest of badgers, none
Could fight with his foemen, three to one.
Into his den he would have fled,
But a shot came—bang—and he fell down dead.

PUSSY.

WHY do you wash yourself, Pussy, I pray,
Every half hour, all through the day?
PUSSY. Because I never can bear to be seen,
If I am not quite neat and quite clean;
From top to toe, head and paws with me,
Must be bright and comely as bright can be.

And very often I heard them tell,
How all petted Pussy, and liked her well;
How she might sleep in the room when she chose,
And e'en on the laps of the ladies might doze;
How our clean little Pussy by all was caress'd,
For her neatness made her a welcome guest.

BOY AND DONKEY.

Boy. Donkey, an ugly creature, thou,
    With ears as tall as a house, I vow.
Donkey. Now, do not for that be cross with me ;
    How can I help how long they be ?
    He who made them must surely know
    Why my ears were created so.

    And as the boy in the world look'd round,
    Many strange things on all sides he found ;
    Some creatures short, and others tall,
    Some that could fly, while others did crawl—
    But he saw with joy, how God's bounteous care
    Was spread over all things, ev'rywhere.

BEAR AND LOG.

" WELL, now, here *is* a wonderful thing !
  This great, huge log to my leg will cling.
  I 'll get rid of you soon, I will ;
  I 'll carry you straight up yonder hill,
  And send you splashing, before I go,
  Into the river that runs below."

The poor old bear he had reckon'd wrong—
  The great log bore him with it along ;
  Over and over he roll'd on the ground
  Till the brains in his head seem'd whirling round.
  He'd thought to free himself, but instead,
  He lay on the ground with the log, half dead.

WOLF AT THE GRATE.

" So, Master Wolf, you're hungry again,
  And therefore to steal a fat sheep are fain ;
  See how they're crowding together, in fear !
  Seize one quickly, Sir Wolf,—d'ye hear ?
  Ah, I perceive, the door is fast,
  And thus, you bad thief, you're baulk'd at last."

All too long at the door stood he,
Watching the sheep so greedily ;
Saw not how two men came that way,
Peasants they were, and sticks had they ;
And the wolf was beaten soundly and well ;
How he got off at all, I ne'er could tell.

LITTLE MOUSE.

" Run, little Mouse, or, I tell you true,
   The cat will soon make an end of you.
   Whisk into your hole, draw in your tail,
   That Puss to catch you once more may fail.
   She's coming; but see, as best she may,
   She's slinking with empty mouth away."

   Of course, I could but be glad, you know,
   That Mousie had thus escaped her foe.
   But much I fear that it will not last:
   Puss has been watching this long time past;
   If Mousie to thieve will sally out,
   She'll pay with her life, some day, no doubt.

CHICKENS.

" CHICKENS, Chickens, wherever ye roam,
Turn about quickly, and run back home.
Hark to your mother who's calling you there,
Look at the hawk that wheels in the air;
To the sheltering roof over yonder fly,
For if he seizes you, you must die."

Trembling beneath the shed they stood,
And the hen ran about in anxious mood,
When a shot from the garden fired they heard,
And headlong down fell the robber bird.
Then to her chicks did the mother call,
And carefully spread her wings o'er them all.

MONKEY AND BOY.

BOY. Up in the apple-tree, what do you do,
        You hideous, ugly Monkey, you?
MONKEY. So you'd laugh at me, Boy, down there;
        I 'll pelt you well, if you don't take care.
BOY. Your rage, good Monkey, is my delight,
        While you fling down apples to show your spite.

        Thus, for a time, the war they waged;
        The monkey shriek'd, he was so enraged;
        To tease him well was the youngster's joy,
        And the monkey's vengeance to pelt the boy,
        Who pick'd up a dozen of apples good,
        And ran off, laughing, as fast as he could.

PIG, DOG, AND COW.

Cow. Dear, what a roaring, and racket, and riot!
Pig there, and Dog, will you never be quiet?
Pig and Dog. Be silent yourself, old Cow, d'ye hear;
When we quarrel, how dare you interfere?
Just you mind your own business, friend;
'T will be the best for you, in the end.

The cow she said nothing in reply,
But went on feeding, quite peacefully;
A quiet life is the best, she thought.
But the others quarrell'd, and bit, and fought,
Till the farmer's man, with his heavy whip,
Came out at the noise, and made them skip.

GOOSE.

" Goose, what a poor little creature are you,
   To have no stockings and never a shoe."
Goose. You might certainly give me a pair;
   But would they be proper for me to wear?
   Would not the beautiful things be soil'd,
   If I went in the water, and wetted, and spoil'd?

The nearest brook was his favourite place;
He went splashing through it with thoughtful pace,
Walking or swimming its surface o'er,
And little caring for anything more.
He stay'd in the water the whole day through,
And never thought once of stocking or shoe.

TWO DOGS.

THE LITTLE ONE. What can you do, sir, pray let me see?
Can you walk on two legs, like me?
Can you beg prettily, dance and spring,
And to your master his slippers bring?
THE BIG ONE. I can't do all that, but care I take
That into the house no thief may break.

Both are good in their way, say I,
If each does his office carefully.
The little one passes the time away
With his merry gambols, and tricks, and play;
But if I should choose between the two,
I'd have the big one; and would not you?

CALF AND DOG.

CALF. Here in the farmyard it's fine to-day;
      Come, little Doggie, and let us play.
  DOG. We will, if you please; now you begin.
      Run out, and I'll try and fetch you in.
CALF. Go, ill-temper'd Dog; it is not right
      To pretend to be playing, and then to bite.

      The calf from that day would make demur,
      When ask'd to play with the surly cur;
      He always play'd false—that the young calf knew,
      And ran whenever he came in view;
      And when one day he bit the calf once more,
      With a kick it roll'd him o'er and o'er.

PUG AND YARD DOG.

PUG. Here, you great clumsy Dog, I say,
　　　Just you run off without delay.
　　　Don't wait till I catch you ; if you do,
　　　It will be so much the worse for you.
YARD DOG. Cease, little brawler, to vent your spleen ;
　　　You know you are saying much more than you mean.

　　　Our great yard dog half turn'd his head,
　　　Hearing scarce what the pug dog said ;
　　　Then Pug directly began to quail,
　　　And ran off quickly with drooping tail.
　　　When he got safe home, but not before,
　　　He barked right valiantly out at the door.

FAREWELL.

AND now we take leave of each good friend,
For here our Fables and Pictures end ;—
One hundred stories you now have heard,
Of men and children, of beast and bird ;
One hundred pictures you here have seen—
To help to show what the stories mean.

Let me ask you, dear children, all and each,
Have you mark'd the lesson these Fables teach ?
It is " To show kindness and gentle care
To all God's creatures, everywhere—
Seeing God's kindness appears display'd
In all the works that His wisdom made."

R. CLAY, PRINTER, LONDON.

www.ingramcontent.com/pod-product-compliance
Lightning Source LLC
Chambersburg PA
CBHW020804020726
47495CB00008B/2586